For Dan.

STERLING CHILDREN'S BOOKS
New York

An Imprint of Sterling Publishing Co., Inc.
1166 Avenue of the Americas
New York, NY 10036

STERLING CHILDREN'S BOOKS and the distinctive Sterling Children's Books logo
are registered trademarks of Sterling Publishing Co., Inc.

ISBN 978-1-4549-3370-0

Distributed in Canada by Sterling Publishing Co., Inc.
c/o Canadian Manda Group, 664 Annette Street Toronto, Ontario M6S 2C8, Canada
Distributed in the United Kingdom by GMC Distribution Services
Castle Place, 166 High Street, Lewes, East Sussex BN7 1XU, England
Distributed in Australia by NewSouth Books, University of New South Wales
Sydney, NSW 2052, Australia

For information about custom editions, special sales, and premium and corporate purchases,
please contact Sterling Special Sales at 800-805-5489 or specialsales@sterlingpublishing.com.

Manufactured in China
Lot #:
2 4 6 8 10 9 7 5 3 1
06/19

sterlingpublishing.com

Cover and interior design
by Jo Obarowski

MUSICAL MAC

BY BRENDAN KEARNEY

STERLING CHILDREN'S BOOKS
New York

Mac is a millipede. He has LOTS of arms and LOTS of legs, which is very handy indeed when there are LOTS of things to do.

The day of the annual Soggy Bog Talent Show had arrived.

Mac had always dreamed of competing, but every year he was TOO shy and TOO scared to enter alone.

This year however, Mac had a BRILLIANT idea.
If I join a band, I won't have to enter on my own! he beamed to himself.

So he packed up his instruments and marched off.

He spotted an orchestra rehearsing in the grass up ahead.
He crept closer and closer and began to play along . . .

"HOLD IT! What are you doing?" asked the conductor.
The orchestra fell silent and everyone looked up at Mac.

"Sorry," Mac replied awkwardly.
"I thought I would join in."

"Well you can't, I'm afraid, because this orchestra is full. You play the violin excellently, but you are FAR TOO BIG for this group, and besides, we don't have any spare jackets!"

Embarrassed, Mac moved on.
I'll find another band, he
thought to himself as . . .

he crept past a log pile,

over a boulder stack,

and into a dark, dark alleyway.

He saw a group practicing under a streetlight ahead.
He tiptoed nearer and nearer and began to play along.

"HOLD IT! Where's that trumpet coming from?" boomed the bandleader.
The band fell silent and everyone looked over at Mac.
"Sorry. I thought I would join in," Mac replied timidly.
"Well you can't, I'm afraid, because there is no trumpet part in this song.
You play the trumpet brilliantly, but you are FAR TOO SMALL for this
jazz band. And besides, you don't even have a hat!"
chuckled the cat.

Mac continued looking for a band to join all morning.

He played guitar with frogs and banged on drums with dogs.

He played flute with bears and even danced with hares.

I'll never play in the Soggy Bog Talent Show,
Mac thought sadly to himself.

As he trudged home, Mac heard a choir singing high up in the trees. *One last try!* he decided as he cautiously climbed higher and higher and began to sing along.

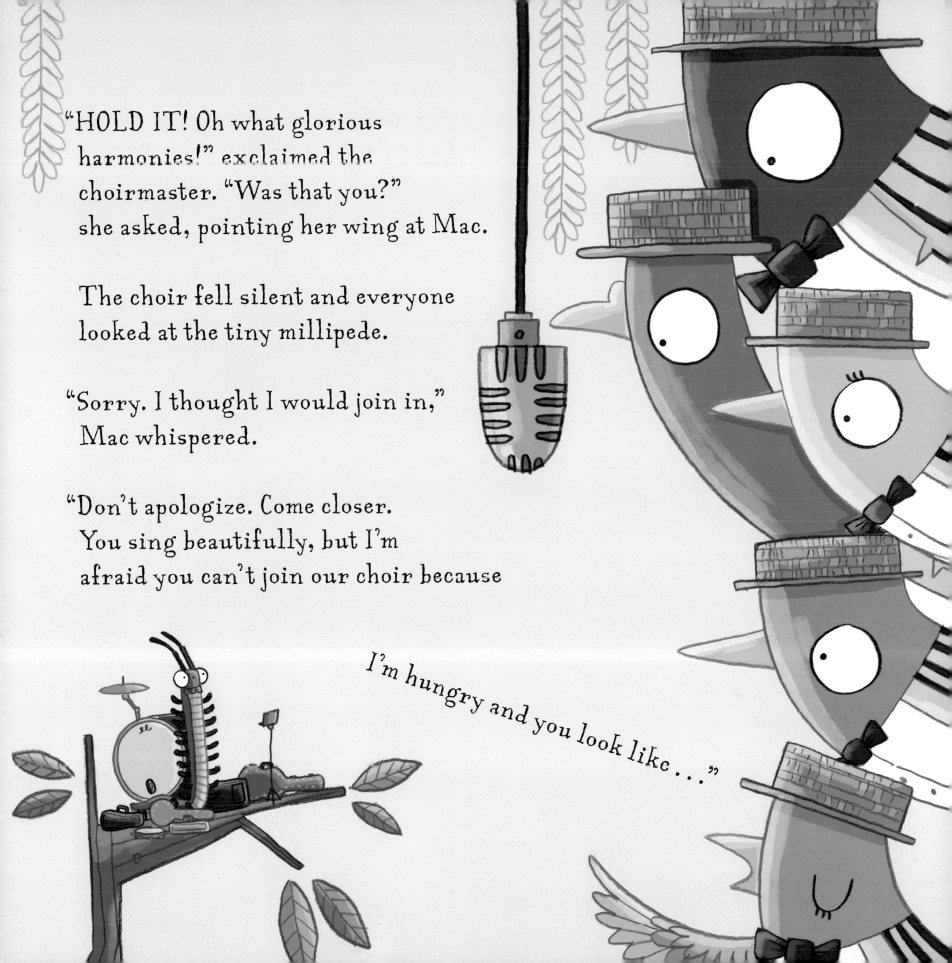

"HOLD IT! Oh what glorious harmonies!" exclaimed the choirmaster. "Was that you?" she asked, pointing her wing at Mac.

The choir fell silent and everyone looked at the tiny millipede.

"Sorry. I thought I would join in," Mac whispered.

"Don't apologize. Come closer. You sing beautifully, but I'm afraid you can't join our choir because

I'm hungry and you look like . . ."

"AHHHHHH!!!!"
Mac ran for his life.

He scrambled through brambles, leapt over lily pads,

and pushed through a large crowd to escape the birds.

"Phew, that was close!" he sighed when he finally stopped to rest.

Suddenly the lights dimmed and a spotlight shined down on Mac.
He was on stage at the Soggy Bog Talent Show. ALONE.

Terrified, he stood motionless. The audience silently stared at him.

But then, one by one, they called out.

He tucked his violin under his chin and strapped his drum to his back.

He grabbed his trumpet and guitar,

and put a tambourine under one of his feet.

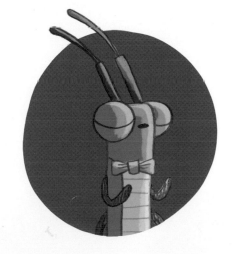

Taking a deep breath, he closed his eyes and hoped for the best.

The crowd erupted with applause, and before long, everyone was cheering, dancing, and singing along.

Mac realized, with the help of his new friends, that playing music on his own wasn't too scary at all. He didn't need to be in a band to be in the Soggy Bog Talent Show. He could just be himself— his very own ONE MAN BAND!

OCT 3 1 2019

DISCARD